John Lydgate

The Childe of Bristow, a Poem

Anatiposi

John Lydgate

The Childe of Bristow, a Poem

Reprint of the original, first published in 1859.

1st Edition 2023 | ISBN: 978-3-38230-698-4

Anatiposi Verlag is an imprint of Outlook Verlagsgesellschaft mbH.

Verlag (Publisher): Outlook Verlag GmbH, Zeilweg 44, 60439 Frankfurt, Deutschland
Vertretungsberechtigt (Authorized to represent): E. Roepke, Zeilweg 44, 60439 Frankfurt, Deutschland
Druck (Print): Books on Demand GmbH, In de Tarpen 42, 22848 Norderstedt, Deutschland

THE

CHILDE OF BRISTOW,

A POEM

BY JOHN LYDGATE.

EDITED,

FROM THE ORIGINAL MS. IN THE BRITISH MUSEUM,

BY

CLARENCE HOPPER.

PRINTED FOR THE CAMDEN SOCIETY.
M.DCCC.LIX.

INTRODUCTION.

THIS interesting little legend, preserved in a volume in the Harleian Collection of MSS. in the British Museum, calendared as "Poems by Chaucer, Dan Lydgate, and others," can hardly be said to have escaped the notice of our antiquaries, since Ritson, in his Bibliographia Poetica, p. 71, mentions it, and gives its authorship to Lydgate.

Beyond this notice I know of no other evidence to establish either the date of the poem or its writer, although its simplicity and beauty would not have been unworthy of the author of the Canterbury Tales, or that voluminous poetaster Dan* John.

The story itself would not appear to be an original idea of the poet, for he says, "I found it written in olde hand."

The scene is laid in Bristol, or rather about seven miles from that city, where dwelt a squire of vast possessions and unbounded wealth, acquired by mal-practices, and wrested from the poor.

A usurer, and an ungodly man, he cared not whom he

* *Dan*, a corruption of *Dom* or *Dam*, the abbreviated form of *Dominus*.

wronged so that he might aggrandise his only son, the " childe of Bristow," desirous that none should surpass him in worldly riches. When his son arrived at the age of twelve, the father took pains to have him well versed in clerkly lore, and desired to give him a year's instruction in the law; but this measure is opposed by the youth, who, in the words of an old saw, thus answers, " They fare full well who learn no law," and announces his determination to follow no other profession than that of "marchantye," and to become bound to a Bristol merchant for seven years. To Bristol accordingly " the childe " goes, and by his courtesy and amiability soon wins the hearts of all who know him. In the mean time, a sudden illness throws the squire on his death-bed, and now the country is sought, far and near, for some one to become his executor. No one will under-take the responsibility of becoming the personal repre-sentative of a man whose wealth had been acquired by means so questionable. In the end, in despair, he sends for his son to undertake the office; compelled by the solemn adjuration of his father, the son accepts the charge, but unwillingly, and upon condition that, in a fortnight after that day on which his father's spirit passed away, he would reappear in that same chamber, that his son might be certified whether his soul were in weal or woe.

After priestly shrift and ghostly consolation the squire expires, and the pious " childe" sells all his chattels and distributes the produce in alms, or expends it in masses for the welfare of his father's soul.

The end of the appointed fortnight arrives, and we see the son kneeling in prayer in the dead chamber for half a day, when suddenly, in lightning and thunder, his father's spirit burning like a living coal, with a fiery chain about his neck, stands before him, led by the Evil One. Being conjured to speak, the wretched man explains that his goods were gotten wrongfully, and that he must expiate his ill doings by one hundred years of torment. The son makes him promise to return in another fortnight, and he will endeavour to bring his soul " in better way."

Overwhelmed with sorrow, next day the son departs for Bristol, and sells his inheritance to his master for three hundred pounds.

Thereupon, he gives notice in church and market that if any person whom his father had wronged would come to him, restitution should be made; and by the fortnight's end all his gold is gone.

While at prayer, as before, the spirit again makes his appearance, but this time without the encircling chain, and black, not burning, but full of care. His state being inquired into, he blesses his son, and relates how his bitter chain had fallen off, and his burning agony had ceased, but he must still dwell in pain until his foredoomed time had been fulfilled. On inquiring what was most against him, he explained that he had omitted the payment of tithes and offerings, and, until they were restored with increase, all prayer would be unavailing.

" The childe" desires another interview at the end of a further fortnight. Forthwith he seeks his master, requesting more gold. The merchant upbraids him with having been given to bad company and gambling, reminds him that all his property is gone, and that he has nought now to sell.

The apprentice hears his reproaches in silence, but offers to become his bond-slave, himself and all his to the world's end, if he will but advance him forty marks. The kindly merchant lends him forty pounds, and " the childe" craves another fortnight's leave of absence.

During this time he makes restitution to all the churches near which his father had dwelt. Going " by the street" he is met by a poor man, who tells him that his father was indebted to him for a seam of corn. The youth sorrowfully exclaims, that his silver and gold are gone, but, stripping off his garments, and putting them upon the poor man, he beseeches him to pray for his father's soul.

Bereft of his gay apparel down " to shirte and breche," he directs his steps into the dead man's chamber to pray as before. Suddenly he hears the sound of music, and perceives a brilliant light. A vision of his father's glorified spirit, in the form of a naked child in angel-hand, appears and blesses him, praying that God will requite his filial endeavours, and assuring him that he is going to eternal happiness.

"The childe" returns thanks to God, and wends his way to Bristol attired as he was. The worthy merchant, astonished at his plight, wishes to know the reason, when he unfolds to him the whole story. Pleased with such exemplary affection, the master makes him his partner, endows him with all his lands, and marries him to the daughter of a worthy man. At the merchant's death he inherits all his possessions.

The moral of this pretty little composition points at the sin of covetousness, and the blessings attendant upon the observation of the fifth commandment. Like Job in the Holy Scriptures, " the childe of Bristowe"

> ' First was riche and sitthen bare,
> And sitthen richer than ever he was.'

An harmonious repetition of the first lines of the poem concludes this simple and unaffected tale.

· C. H.

London, March, 1859.

THE CHILDE OF BRISTOW.

1 He that made bothe heuene and hell,[a]
  man and woman, in dayes vij,
  and alle shal fede and fille ;
  he graunte us alle his blessyng,
  more and lasse, bothe olde and yong,
  that herkeneth and hold hem stille.

2 The beste songe that ever was made
  ys not worth a lekys blade,
  but men wol tende y^r till ;
  ther for y pray you in y^s place
  of your talking y^t ye be pes,
  yf it be your wille.

3 I found it writen in olde hand,
  that som tyme dwellid in England
  a squyer mykel of myght;
  he had castels, tounes, and toures,
  feyr forestis and feldes w^t floures,
  beestis wilde and wight.

---

[a] Here evidently must be an error in the transcript. To complete the rhythm it should read, " He that made bothe hell and heuene."—*Vide* last stanza.

4 To lawe he went a gret while,
   pore men he lerned to begile
   all agayns the right;
   mykel good he gadred togedir,
   all w^t treson and dedis lether;
   he drad not god almyght.

5 The good he gadred togeder than
   he had it of many a pore man,
   the most partye w^t wrong:
   he had a sone shuld be his heyre,
   of shap he was semely and feyre,
   of lymes large and long.

6 So moche his mynde was on y^t chylde
   he rought not whom begiled,
   worldly good to fong;
   and al to make his sone so riche
   that non other myght hym be liche,
   so ment he ever among.

7 When the child was xij yere and more
   his fader put hym unto lore
   to lerne to be a clerke;
   so long he lernyd in clergie,
   til he was wise and wittye,
   and drad all dedis derke.

8 The fader seid to his sone dere,
   "to lawe thu shalt go a yere,
   and coste me xx marke;
   for ever the better thu shalt be,
   ther shall no man be gile the
   neyther in worde ne werke."

9 The child answerd w^t a soft sawe;
   "they fars ful well y^t lerne no lawe,
   and so y hope to do;
   that lyue wil y never lede,
   to put my soule in so gret drede,
   to make god my foo. /

10 To sle my soule it wer routhe;
   any science that is trouthe
   y shall amytte me ther to ;
   for to forsake my soule helthe
   for any wynnyng of worldes welthe,
   that will y never do. /

11 Hit hath ever be myn avise
   to lede my lyf by marchandise,
   to lerne to bye and selle;
   that good getyn by marchantye,
   it is trouthe, as thenketh me,
   ther w^t will I melle.

12 Here at Bristow dwelleth on
   is held right a juste trew man,
   as y here now telle ;
   his prentys will y be vij yer,
   his science truly for to lere
   and w^t hym will y dwelle."

13 The squyer unto Bristow rade,
   and w^t the marchand cownant made,
   vij yere to have his sone;
   he gaf hym gold gret plenté,
   the child his prentys shuld be,
   his science for to conne.

14 The child toke ful wel to lore,
 his love was in god evermore;
 as it was his wone,
 he wax so curteise and bolde,
 all merchantȝ loued hym, yong and olde,
 that in that contré gan wone.

15 Leue we now that child thore,
 and of his fader speke we more,
 that was so stoute and bolde;
 he was avaunced so hye,
 there was no man in yᵗ contré
 durst don but as he wolde.

16 And ever he usid usery,
 he wold not lene but he wyst why
 avauntage dobell tolde;
 tethynges he liste never to pay,
 yf parsons and vicares wold oght say
 he uewid hem cares colde.

17 All thyng wol end atte last;
 god on hym soche sekenes cast,
 he myght no leng abide;
 but on his ded bed he lay,
 and drow toward his endyng day;
 for al his power and pride.

18 Then he sent for knyghtes and squyers,
 which were his comperys
 in that contré be syde:
 he seid emonges hem everych on,
 "sires, my lyf is ner gone;
 hit may not be denyede."

19 Ther was no man in y^t contré
   that his executo^r wold be,
   nor for no good ne ill:
   they seid his good was geten so
   they wold not have y^r w^t to do,
   for drede of god in heuen.

20 He prayed hem, and they seid nay;
   allas! he seid, and welaway!
   w^t a rufull stevyn:
   after hissone son he sent,
   evyn to Bristow vereament,
   was thens but myles vij.

21 The child to chamber toke his way;
   ther his fader on ded bed lay,
   and asked hym of his chere:
   " sone, (he sed,) wel come to me;
   y ly here now, as y^u may se;
   my endyng day negheth nere.

22 But, sone, thu must be myn heyre
   of al my londes good and faire,
   and my lordships fer and ner;
   ther for, sone, now y pray the,
   myn atto^{r}ney that thu be,
   when y am broght to bere."

23 The child answerd w^t wordes mylde;
   " ye se, fader, y am but a childe;
   discrecion haue y none,
   to take soche a charge on me,
   by my faith! that shal not be;
   y can no skyle ther on.

24 Here ben knyghtes and squyers,
   which were yor compers,
   and many a worthy man;
   yf y shuld soche on me take,
   that alle these worthi men forsake,
   a fole then wer y one."

25 He seid, " y haue no sone but the,
   and myn heire y^u most nedis be;
   ther may no man sey nay;
   moche good haue y gadred to geder
   w^t extorcion and dedis lither,
   alas and welaway!

26 All this, sone, y gadred for the,
   and thu so sone failest me
   at my nedeful day;
   frendship, sone, is yll to triste,
   eche man be ware of had y wiste,
   god wote, so may I sey."

27 " Sone, (he seid,) thu scapest not so;
   that shalt y^u weten, or thu go;
   he then charge y the
   to fore god thu mothe answer,
   and as thu wilt my blessyng ber,
   myn atto^rney that thu be."

28 " A fader, ye bynde me w^t a charge,
   and y shal bynde yow w^t as large
   as ye bynde now me:
   the same day fortenyght y^t ye passe,
   y charge yow appere in this place,
   yor spiret lat me se.

29 For ye haue bound me so sare,
  now y most nedis, how ever y fare,
  do your comaundement;
  ther for y charge yow y^t ye appere,
  that y may se yŏ soule here,
  whethir it be saued or shent!

30 And that ye do no scathe to me,
  ne none, that shal come w^t the."
  " sone, (he seid,) y assent,
  but, allas, that y was born;
  that man is soule shuld be lorn
  for my golde or rent."

31 Al thyng most ende atte last,
  god soche sekenys on hym cast,
  that he most nedys go :
  the parish prest up was soght ;
  the glĩose sacment w^t hym he broght,
  that dyed for mannys woo.

32 Ther he shrove hym w^t hert sore,
  and cryed god mercy ever more !
  as it was tyme to do;
  when god wold, he went his way ;
  his sones song was " welaway !"
  for hym his hert was wo.

33 His sone sought fro toun to toun
  for prestis and men of religioun
  the *Dirige* for to say :
  an C prestis he had and mo;
  gret yeftys he gaf them tho,
  chargyng hem for his fader to pray.

34 Yong children had gret hole,
   and pore wym̃en had gret dole,
   that holpe hym not a day;
   and sitthe broght hym in his pytt,
   as al men must, thei may not flyt,
   whether thei wel or nay.

35 When thei had broght hym in his graue,
   his sone y^t thoght his soule to saue,
   yf god wold gef hym leue;
   al the catel his fader hade,
   he sold it up and money made,
   and labored morow and eve.

36 He sought aboute in that contré tho,
   wher any almes myght be do,
   and largely he dyd hem yeue
   wayes and brugges for to make,
   and pore men for goddes sake
   he yeaf hem gret releve.

37 Who so axed aght, he made her pay,
   and xxx^ti trental of masses he let say
   for his fadres sake;
   he let never til he had bewared
   all the treso^r his fader spared
   a seth to god for to make.

38 By y^t day fortenyghtes ende was come;
   his gold was gon all and some;
   (many one of hym spake)
   and al thynges that wer meuable,
   he gaf aboute, w^t outen fable,
   to.pore men that wold take.

39 By than the fourtenyght was broght to ende,
 the child to the chamber gan wende,
 wher his fader dyed;
 a doun he knelid half a day;
 al the good prayers y^t he couthe say,
 his fader for to abide.

40 Be twene mydday and under
 y^r came a blast of lightnyng and dunder
 thurgh the walles wide;
 as al the place on fire had be;
 the child seid, " *Benedicite !* "
 and fast on god he cryde.

41 And as he sate on his prayere,
 sone be fore hym gan appere,
 foule tydynges be twene,
 his faders soule brennyng as glede,
 the deuel by ye nekke gan hym lede
 in a brennyng cheyne.

42 This child seid, " I côiure the,
 what so ever y^u be, speke to me;"
 that other answerd a geyne:
 " y am thi fader that y^e be gate;
 now thu may se of myn a state;
 lo! how y dwelle in peyne."

43 The child seid, "ful woo is me,
 in this plite that yow se;
 it persheth myn hert sore;"
 " sone, (he seid,) thus am y led,
 for be cause of my falshed
 that y used ever more.

44 Mi good was getyn wrongfully;
   but it myght restord be,
   and a seth be made ther fore;
   an C yer thus shal y do,
   gef me my trouthe I wer ago,
   for till than my soule is lore."

45 " Nay, fader, that shal not be;
   in better plite y wol yow se,
   yf god wol gef me grace;
   but ye shal me yor trouthe plighte
   this same day fourtenyght
   ye shal appere in this place.

46 And y shal labo^{r}e, yf y may,
   to bryng yor soule in better way,
   yf y haue lyf and space."
   he graunted hym in gret hast;
   w^t that ther cam a donder blast,
   and bothe ther way gan passe.

47 The child had neuer so gret sorwe;
   he rose up apon the morwe,
   to Bristow gan he wende;
   to his mayster he gan say,
   " y haue serued yow many a day;
   for goddes loue be my frend.

48 My fader out of this world is past;
   y am come to yow in hast;
   y haue euer founde yow kynde;
   me nedith a litel some of gold;
   myn heritage shal be sold,
   croppe, rote, and rynde."

49 His maister sed, " what nede wer the
  to selle thy thrift so hastely ?
  it wer not for thy prow ;
  yf thu any bargeyn haue boght,
  for gold ne siluer care y^u noght ;
  y shal lene the right y now.

50 An C mark yf thu wilt haue,
  this vij. yer y wil neuer craue ;
  wher for avise the now ;
  for yf thu selle thyn heritage
  that shuld ye holpe in thi yong age,
  an unwise man art thow."

51 " Gramercy ! (he seid,) maister hende,
  this was a proffer of a frende ;
  but truly it shal be sold ;
  better chepe ye shal it have
  then any man, so god me saue,
  for nedys y must haue gold."

52 He seid, " what is it worth by yer ?"
  " ane C marke of money cler ;
  the stuward this me tolde."
  " then shal y gef the iij.C pound,
  every penny hole and round ; "
  the yong [man] seid, " y holde.

53 Dere mayster, y yow pray,
  haue her dedis,—foch me my pay ;
  for y must houe agayn ;
  y haue to do in soundre place,
  y pray yow, of fourtenyght space
  y shal yow quytte certayn."·

54 His mayster loued hym so wele,
   he fette hym gold euery dele;
   than was ye child ful fayn:
   he toke his good, and gan to go;
   and for his fader his hert was woo,
   that bode in so mykel payn.

55 His sone lete crie al aboute
   in churches and markettes, w^t oute doute,
   wher his fader dud wone;
   wher his fader dud destriccion
   to man or woman in any toun,
   they shuld come to his sone.

56 And he shal make a seth ther fore,
   and his good ayen restore,
   eche man his porcion;
   ever as they come, he made her pay,
   and charged hem for his fader pray,
   in blisse that he might wone.

57 By that the fourtenyght was come,
   his gold was gon al and some;
   then had he ne more:
   in to the chamber he went y^t tide,
   the same that his fader in dyde,
   and knelid as he dud ore.

58 And, as he sate in his prayer,
   the spiret be fore hym gan apper,
   right as he dud be fore;
   saue ye cheyn away was caught;
   blak he was, but he brent noght,
   but yet he was in care.

59 " Wel come, fader, (seid the childe ;)
    y pray yow w^t wordes mylde,
    tel me of your astate."
    " sone, (he seid,) the better for the,
    y blessid mote the tyme be,
    that euer I the be gate.

60 Thou hast releuyd me of moche wo :
    my bitter chayne is fal me fro,
    and the fire so hote ;
    but yet dwel y stille in peyn,
    and euer must, in certeyn,
    tyl I haue fulfilled my day."

61 " Fader, (he seid,) I charge yow tel me
    what is moste ayens the,
    and doth yow most disese?"
    " tethynges and offrynges, sone, (he sayd,)
    for y them neuer truly payd,
    wherfor my peynes may not cesse :

62 But it be restored agayn
    to as many churches in certayn,
    and also mykel encresse,
    all that for me thu dos pray,
    helpeth me not, to the uttermost day,
    the valure of a pese.

63 Ther for, sone, y pray the
    gef me my trouthe y left w^t the,
    and let me wynde my way."
    " nay, fader, (he seid,) ye gete it noght,
    another craft ther shal be soght,
    yet efte y will assay ;

64 But yor trouthe ye shal me plight,
   this same day a fourtenyght
   ye shal come ageyn to yor day;
   ye shall appere her in this place,
   and y shal loke, w.^t goddes grace,
   to amend yow, yf y may."

65 The spiret went forth in his way;
   the childe rose up that other day;
   for no thyng wold he lette:
   even to Bristowe gan he wynde;
   ther he mette w^t his maister kynde;
   wel goodly he hym grette.

66 " When y haue nede y come to yow,
   mayster, but ye helpe me now;
   in sorwe my herte is sette;
   me nedeth a litel sume of gold;
   another bargeyn make y wold;"
   and w^t that word he wepte.

67 His maister seid, " y^u art a fole;
   thu has ben at som bad scole;
   by my fecth y hold the mad;
   for thu has played atte dice,
   or at som other games nyce,
   and lost vp sone y^t thu had.

68 Thu hast right noght y^t y^u may selle;
   all is gon, as y here telle;
   thi gouernaunce, sone, is bad."
   then he seid until his maister fre,
   " myn owne bodye y wil selle to the,
   for euer to be thy lad.

69 Bonde to the y will me bynde,
   me and alle myne, to yᵉ worldes ende,
   to helpe me in this nede."
   he seid, " how mykel woldest yᵘ haue? "
   " xl mark, and ye wold foche saue,
   for that shuld do my dede.

70 I hope that shal my cares kele."
   the burger louyd yᵉ child so wele,
   that to his chamber he yede;
   xl pound he gan hym brynge:
   " sone, her is more than thyn askyng;—
   almyghti god the spede!"

71 " Gramercy! sire, (gan he say,)
   god yow quytte that best may!
   and trewe ye shal me fynde;
   y have to do a thyng or two,
   a fourtenyght gef me lef to go,
   y have euer founde yow kynde."

72 He gaf hym leue; he went his way;
   but on his fader he thoght ay,
   he goth not out of mynde;
   he sought alle yᵉ churches in yᵗ contré,
   wher his fader had dwellid by,
   he left not one be hynde.

73 He made a seth wᵗ hem echon;
   by yᵗ tyme his gold was gon,
   they couthe aske hym no mare;
   saue as he went by yᵉ strete,
   wᵗ a pore man gan he mete,
   al most naked and bare.

74 " Your fader oweth me for a zeme of corn."
   down he knelid him be forn.
   " for yoʳ faders soules sake;
   and y hym drad ful sare,
   som amendes to me ye make,
   for hym that Marie bare."

75 " Welaway ! (seid yᵉ yong man,)
   for my gold and siluer is gan;
   y haue not for to pay :"—
   of his clothes he gan take,
   and put hem on yᵉ pore manis bake,
   chargyng for his fader to pray.

76 Hosen and shon he gaue hym tho;
   in sherte and breche he gan go ;
   he had no clothes gay,
   in to the chamber he went yᵗ tide,
   the same yᵗ his fader on dyde,
   and knelid half a day.

77 When he had knelid and prayed long,
   hym thoght he herd yᵉ myriest song
   yᵗ any erthely man myght here ;
   after the song, he saw a light,
   as thow a thousant torches bright,
   it shone so faire and clere.

78 In that light, so faire lemand,
   a naked child in angel hand
   be fore hym dud appere;
   and seid, " sone, blessid thu be,
   and all yᵗ euer shall come of the,
   that euer thu goten were."

79 " Fader, (he seid,) ful wel is me,
    in that plite that y yow se;
    y hone that ye be saue."
    " sone, (he seid,) y go to blisse;
    god almyghti quyte the this !
    thi good ageyn to haue ;

80 Thu has made the ful bare
    to aqueynche me of mykel care,
    my trouthe, good sone, y craue."
    " haue yor trouthe (he seid) fre,
    and of thi blessyng I pray the,
    yf that ye wold foche saue."

81 " In that blessyng mote y^u wone,
    that our lady gaf here sone,
    and myn on the y lay."
    now that soule is gon to blisse
    w^t moche ioye and angelis,
    more then y can say.

82 This child thanked god almyght
    and his moder Marye bryght,
    when he sey that aray;
    euen to Bristow gan he gon
    in his sherte and breche allon;
    hed he no clothes gay.

83 When y^s burges ye child gan se,
    he seid then, " *Benedicite !*
    sone, what araye is this ? "
    " truly, maister, (seid ye childe,)
    y am come me to yelde
    as your bonde man.".

84 The burges seid anon right,
  " me mervayleth mykel of ye sight;
  tel me now how it ys."
  "whatsom euer ye put me to,
  after my power it shall be do,
  while my lyf wil laste."

85 "For ye loue be twene vs hath be,
  tell me, sone, how it stant wt the;
  why thu gos in this way:"
  " Sir, al my good y haue sold, y wys,
  to gete my fader to heuene blys;
  for sothe as y yow say.

86 For ther was no man but y,
  that wold be his attorny
  at his endyng day."
  tho he told hym further,
  how ofte he dud his fader appere,
  and eke in what aray.

87 " And now his soule into blisse
  y sey hym led wt angelis;
  almyghti god the yelde !
  for thurf your good he is saue,
  and his dere blessyng y haue,
  and al my cares be kelde."

88 " Sone, (he seid,) blessed mote yu be,
  that so pore woldest make the,
  thy faders soule to saue;
  to speke ye honor may al mankynde;
  thu art a tristy siker frende;
  soche fynde y but silden;

89 But fewe sones ben of tho,
   that wol serue her fader so,
   when he is hens gon;
   certes fynd y many on,
   but none soche as y^u art on;
   by my fecth y leve not on."

90 Hys maister seid, " y shal ye tell,
   thu canst both bye and sell;
   here now make y the
   myn owne felow in al wise
   of worldly good and merchandise,
   for thy trouthe so fre.

91 Al so, sone, y haue no childe
   myn heritage for to wilde,
   goten of my body;
   here y make the now myn heyr
   of alle my landes good and faire,
   and myn attorney that y^u be."

92 His maister dud hym weddid be
   to a worthy manis doghter of y^t contré
   with ioye and grete solace;
   and when his mayster was ded,
   in to all his good he entred,
   landes, catell, and place.

93 Thus hath y^s yong man keuered care;
   first was riche and sitthen bare,
   and sitthen richer then euer he was :—
   now he y^t made both helle and heuene,
   and all the worlde in dayes seuene,
   graunte vs alle his grace.
                      Amen.

GLOSSARY.

abide, *make atonement for, expiate.*
amytte, *apply.*
asseth, *satisfaction.*
ayen, ayens, *against.*
bere, *burial*
bewared, *expended.*
brennyng, *burning.*
brugges, *bridges.*
but, *unless.*
can (ken), *know.*
chepe, *bargain.*
conne, *learn.*
disese, *to trouble, to annoy.*
districcion (destruction), *injury.*
dole, *grief.*
dunder, *thunder.*
efte, *again.*
ever amonge, *always.*
fayn, *glad.*
foch save, *vouchsafe.*
fong (or fang), *to seize.*
glede, *a live coal.*
hende, *gentle.*
hissone (his'n), *his own.*
hole (howl), *lamentation.*
hone, *to long for.*
houe (hove), *to move.*
kele, kelde, *cool, cooled.*
keuered (covered), *recovered.*
lemand, *glittering.*
lene, *lend.*
lether, lither, *wicked.*

lette, *omit.*
leve, *abbrev. for believe.*
lore, *lost, undone.*
melle (meddle), *mix.*
mothe, *must.*
nyce, *foolish.*
ore (*pro* yore), *formerly.*
pese, *pea.*
prow, *profit.*
quytte, *abbrev. for requite.*
rought, *preterite of to reck.*
routhe, *pity.*
shent, *ruined.*
siker (secure), *safe.*
sitthen, *afterwards.*
stevyn, *groan.*
tende, *abbrev. for attend.*
tho, *then.*
thurf, *through.*
trental, *thirty masses or 30 days of masses.*
treson (trahison), *grasping.*
trouthe, *honest.*
trouthe (troth), *pledge.*
vereament, *truly.*
valure, *value.*
welaway, *an exclamation of woe.*
weten, *know.*
wight, *lively, sprightly.*
wone, *dwell.*
wone (wont), *custom.*
yede (hied), *went.*
zeme (seam), *a quarter of corn.*